VALENTINE'S DAY, HERE I COME!™

I ♥ Nily—DJS

With love to all my family & friends—LS

GROSSET & DUNLAP
An imprint of Penguin Random House LLC, New York

First published in the United States of America by Grosset & Dunlap,
an imprint of Penguin Random House LLC, New York, 2022

Text Copyright © 2022 by D. J. Steinberg
Illustrations copyright © 2022 by Penguin Random House LLC

GROSSET & DUNLAP is a registered trademark of Penguin Random House LLC.

Visit us online at penguinrandomhouse.com.

Library of Congress Cataloging-in-Publication Data is available.

Manufactured in China

ISBN 9780593387177   10 9 8 7 6 5 4 3 2 1 HH

VALENTINE'S DAY, HERE I COME!™

BY D. J. STEINBERG

ILLUSTRATED BY LAURIE STANSFIELD

GROSSET & DUNLAP

VALENTINE'S DAY, HERE I COME!

I've got so many cards to write—
a card for everyone.
My friends' names go where it says *TO:* _____.
Mine goes where it says *FROM:* _____.

Yeeesh! I might be up all night
to get all these valentines done!
But I can't wait for tomorrow, 'cause . . .
Valentine's Day, here I come!

5

DRESS-UP RULES

On Valentine's Day,
it's a law, I think,
you can only wear *red*
or *purple* or *pink*!

BREAKFAST SPECIAL

On all other days, Dad's pancakes are round,
and we like them when they are perfectly browned.
But on Valentine's, Dad makes them velvety red,
and—*look!* Just today, they're all heart-shaped instead!

WE LOVE ♥s

We ♥ Valentine's Day.
We ♥ it the minute it starts!
We ♥ it *all* day 'cause as you can see,
we ♥ drawing oodles of ♥s!

8

MY LACY HEART

I'm not so great with scissors
and my cutting's not too steady,
which could be why my lacy heart
looks more like confetti!

ROSES ARE RED

Roses are red.

Violets are blue.

I made you a valentine with stickers and ribbons and glitter and gems
and doilies and petals and sequins and
feathers and buttons and pom-poms and glue!

CUPCAKE CHAOS

There once was a girl named Bess
who tried to bake cupcakes, I guess.
With eggs on the chair
and flour in her hair,
all she made was a horrible mess.

Bess's mother came in with a mop.
Soon the room got cleaned bottom to top.

Mom said, "Come with me
to the cupcakery,"
and they bought them instead at the shop!

PARTY TIME

Out the window, there they are . . .
Moms and dads are parking cars,
Carrying treats all pink and heart-y.
Hooray! They're here for our Valentine's party!

We've waited so long for today.
It's time to put school stuff away
and bring out plates all full of yummies.
What a great day for our *tummies*!

LITTLE CANDY HEARTS

Emily's says "I ♥ You."
Ethan's says "Be Mine."
Theresa's says "You're Groovy"
and Youngmee's says "You Shine."
Benjamin got "Hot Stuff!"
Chantal got "Cutie Pie."
Monique's says "Little Angel."
So . . . how come I got "*Wise Guy*"?!

17

SPECIAL DELIVERY

One valentine goes by my
pet hamster's wheel.

I give one to Sir Fluffy,
my favorite stuffed seal.

Here's one for our guard, who
helps us cross the street.

And for my school friends,
I put one at each seat.

Here are two valentines for
my sister and brother

and the biggest of all for
my father and mother!

A CHOCOLATE MYSTERY

Hello there, Little Chocolate.
What's inside your shell?
Hazelnut or buttercrunch?
How's a kid to tell?
Please do not be cherry
or some yucky kind of cream.
If you are rum raisin,
I may run away and scream.
Here goes . . . I take a nibble.
I try hard to be brave.
Ooh! What's this? Could it be . . .
CARAMEL COCONUT—my fave!

PUPPY DOG TREATS

We love to bake biscuits from bananas and beets,
because puppy dogs *also* deserve special treats!

WARNING!

Cupid is a guy with wings
some people think is cute.
He's got a bow and arrows
that he just can't wait to shoot.
They're magical *love* arrows—*blech!*

So look out up above!
Better run and hide or else
you might end up in *love!!!*

VALENTINE JOKES

Hear the one about the peanut
who sent a card to the cashew?
Guess what the note inside said . . .
It said "I'm NUTS for you!"

Hear the one about the kitty
whose card was very clever?
Guess what the note inside said . . .
It said "Best friends FUR-ever!"

Hear the one about the bee
who sent a valentine?
Guess what the note inside said . . .
Why, of course it said "BEE mine!"

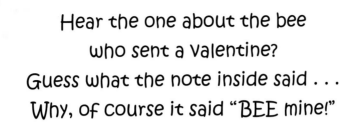

KISSES VS. KISSES

I like kisses that come in a bag—
not the kind that are smoochy and wet—
'cause the chocolatey ones all wrapped up in foil
are the very best kisses to get!

HAPPY *SNIFFLE* VALENTINE'S DAY

I'm wheezy and I'm sneezy.
Look how sniffly my nose is.
I love this day, except that
I'm *allergic* to the roses!

SECRET ADMIRER

A vase of red roses came for Mom—
special delivery.
It was signed "From your Secret Admirer."
Now who in the world could that be?

Secret
Admirer

I run to tell my daddy.
"Hmmm," he says. "Who do you think?"
I shrug, but just then the case is solved
when I see my daddy wink!

THE LAST COOKIE

One last pink cookie's on the plate . . .
what's a kid to do?
Everyone knows they're no good anymore
once Valentine's Day is through!

BEE MINE!

Ask an adult for help cutting out this valentine!